## ALSO BY SJÓN

# MOONSTONE

MOONSTONE

# MOONSTONE

## THE BOY WHO NEVER WAS

# SJÓN

TRANSLATED FROM THE ICELANDIC BY VICTORIA CRIBB

FARRAR, STRAUS AND GIROUX   NEW YORK

Farrar, Straus and Giroux
18 West 18th Street, New York 10011

Copyright © 2013 by Sjón
Translation copyright © 2016 by Victoria Cribb
All rights reserved
Printed in the United States of America
Originally published in Icelandic in 2013 by JPV Publishing, Iceland,
    as *Mánasteinn: Drengurinn sem aldrei var til*
English translation published in the United States by Farrar, Straus
    and Giroux
First American edition, 2016

Owing to limitations of space, permissions acknowledgments appear
on page 147.

Library of Congress Cataloging-in-Publication Data
Names: Sjón, 1962– author. | Cribb, Victoria, translator.
Title: Moonstone : the boy who never was / Sjón ; translated from the
    Icelandic by Victoria Cribb.
Other titles: Mánasteinn: drengurinn sem aldrei var til. English
Description: First American edition. | New York : Farrar, Straus
    and Giroux, 2016.
Identifiers: LCCN 2015037595 | ISBN 9780374212438 (hardcover) |
    ISBN 9780374712877 (e-book)
Classification: LCC PT7511.S62 M3613 2016 | DDC 839/.6935—dc23
LC record available at http://lccn.loc.gov/2015037595

Designed by Jonathan D. Lippincott

Our books may be purchased in bulk for promotional,
educational, or business use. Please contact your local
bookseller or the Macmillan Corporate and Premium Sales
Department at 1-800-221-7945, extension 5442, or by e-mail at
MacmillanSpecialMarkets@macmillan.com.

www.fsgbooks.com
www.twitter.com/fsgbooks • www.facebook.com/fsgbooks

10  9  8  7  6  5  4  3  2  1

To slip into your shadow under cover of night.
To follow your footsteps, your shadow at the window.
That shadow at the window is you and no one else;
    it's you.
Do not open that window behind whose curtains
    you're moving.
Shut your eyes.
I'd like to shut them with my lips.
But the window opens and the breeze, the breeze
which strangely balances flame and flag surrounds my
    escape
with its cloak.
The window opens: it's not you.
I knew it all along.

—Robert Desnos

# I

(October 12–13, 1918)

# i

The October evening is windless and cool. There is a distant throb of a motorcycle. The boy puts his head on one side to get a better fix on the sound. Holding it still, he tries to work out the distance; to hear if the bike is coming closer or moving away; if it's being ridden over level or marshy ground, or up the stony slope on the town side of the hill.

A low groan escapes the man standing over the kneeling boy. With his back pressed to the cliff, the man appears to have merged with his own shadow, become grafted to the rock. He groans again, louder, in increasing frustration, thrusting his hips so his swollen member slides to and fro in the boy's mouth.

The boy expels a breath through his nose. He sucks the penis more firmly between his lips and resumes the rhythmic back-and-forth movements of his head. But he does so more slowly, more quietly, than before, alternately rubbing the dome of the cock against his soft palate and wrapping his tongue around its shaft. That way he can do both at once: fellate the man and listen. He's good at identifying the model by ear. There aren't that many bikes in Iceland, after all, and their owners have taken to tuning them according to their own ideas in the hope of coaxing more power out of them. This could well be an Indian: the stroke of its engine is sharper than a Harley-Davidson's.

He closes his eyes. Yes, not just any Indian but *the* Indian. It's for this that he has studied the sounds; to distinguish this one from all the rest. He's sure now that the motorcycle is drawing nearer, approaching up the slope. In no time at all it will breast the crown of the hill, from where the ground falls away to the eastern edge, beneath which is the cliff and he himself on his knees, with the "gentleman" in his mouth.

The man pushes against the movements of the boy's head, which tells the boy he's close to finishing. As he sucks, he grips the man's cock in his hand and rubs it fast, in time to the throbbing of the engine, tightening his grip whenever the bike accelerates and the engine sings. It has the desired effect. The man presses himself harder against the cliff. Mumbled words escape from between his clenched teeth; snatches of the lewd scenes he is staging in his mind.

The counterpoint between the ever-louder throbbing of the engine and the movements of head and hand causes the boy's flesh to stiffen as well. And although he had been intending to save himself this evening, he cannot resist slipping his free hand into his trouser pocket and stroking himself in time to his servicing of the man.

From the summit of the hill comes an infernal roar. The man is now groaning frantically, in competition with the engine noise.

Is she going over?

The question flashes through the boy's mind, but he has no time to wait for an answer: the penis swells abruptly in his mouth. He pinches the root with his fingers and evades the man's hand as it fumbles for the back of his neck to press him close. When the boy releases his grip, the semen spurts onto the withered leaves of the small willow that is waiting out the winter there.

The motorcycle skids to a halt on the brink. Dirt and gravel rain down on man and boy. With a stifled cry, the man peels himself and his shadow from the cliff face. He begins buttoning his fly with trembling hands, glancing around for an escape route. The boy rises to his feet and steps into the man's path. He is a head taller than the gentleman. Without a word the man flings a crumpled banknote at him and hastens away in the direction of town. The boy smooths out the note and grins; there are two of them, a whole fifteen krónur.

On top of the cliff the Indian's engine shuts off.

Silence falls.

## ii

She appears on the brink like a goddess risen from the depths of the sea, silhouetted against the backdrop of a sky ablaze with the volcanic fires of Katla; a girl like no other, dressed in a black leather overall that accentuates every detail it is intended to hide, with black gloves on her hands, a domed helmet on her head, goggles over her eyes, and a black scarf over her nose and mouth.

The girl pulls down the scarf and pushes up the goggles onto her helmet. Her lips are as red as blood, her eyes ringed with kohl that makes her powdered skin appear whiter than white.

Sólborg Gudbjörnsdóttir, Sóla G—.

The boy whispers:

—I knew it!

His lips form the name of her double:

—Musidora . . .

◆

It's been more than a year since the boy discovered this girl. As if for a split second he had been granted X-ray vision and could see her as she really was.

He had already known her name, where she lived, who her parents were, the company she kept—for they are contemporaries, and in a town of fifteen thousand those of the same age cannot help but be aware of one another—but her world was quite out of reach, far above his rung of society, so he had paid no more attention to her than to others of her kind.

He had made his discovery at a Saturday matinee screening of *The Vampires* at the Old Cinema. He was sitting in his usual spot, feeling irked by the whispers and giggles emanating from a group of kids his own age in the better seats in front. But just as he was about to yell at them to pipe down, people were here to enjoy the film, not the noisy petting of bourgeois brats, he heard one of the girls say she was fed up with ruining the show for the others.

It was when the girl stood up to leave that it happened. The instant her shadow fell on the screen they merged—she and the character in the film. She looked around and the beam of light projected Musidora's features onto her own.

The boy froze in his seat. They were identical.

◆

The boy hears a call from the top of the cliff:

—Máni Steinn Karlsson, I know you're there!

He retreats farther into the willow scrub.

The girl draws a red scarf from the pocket of her overall, throws it over the cliff, and watches it float down to earth. She lingers. But when it becomes clear that the boy is not going to give in, she bursts out laughing and turns on her heel.

The motorcycle starts up and she rides away.

The boy emerges from his hiding place. He picks up the scarf and raises it to his nose. The silky-soft material is still warm from the girl's body, still redolent of feminine sweetness.

—O Sóla G— . . .

# iii

The boy heads homeward over the marsh. As he nears the first houses, he makes a detour west around Skóla-varda Hill and up Njardargata so no one will be able to tell where he's coming from.

At the top of the street he pauses by the northern wall of the Einar Jónsson Sculpture Gallery and peers around the corner. Although it's past midnight, there's still a small crowd gathered on the hill to watch the Katla eruption: drunkards, policemen, laborers, newspaper reporters, university men armed with telescopes, three women, a poet with a hip flask, and waifs and strays like himself.

The gathering is free from the rowdiness that usually attends any congregation of this group after sunset—they emit no shrieks or gusts of singing. When not conversing in low voices they gaze intently at the light show in the east, where the volcano is painting the night sky every shade of red, from scarlet through violet to crimson, before exploding the canvas with flares of bonfire yellow and gaseous blue.

The boy watches the figures. From where he is standing he cannot see what they see. He draws the red scarf from his pocket. The shiny fabric slips through his fingers like quicksilver, red as her lips, red as her motorcycle, red as the ferment in his blood.

The red of the scarf is the only color that matters to him tonight; his whole world is red.


In a three-story house on Midstræti the boy climbs up to the attic, which is home to himself and his great-grandmother's sister. It is kitchen, parlor, and two bedrooms, all rolled into one. He makes his way to his bed, timing his footsteps to the old lady's regular intakes of breath.

Noiselessly he undresses and lies down under the covers. He puts on the scarf, though the old lady has told him many times that it's certain death to sleep with anything around your neck. She knows countless tales of people who have hanged themselves in their sleep.

But the boy is sixteen now; he does what he likes. If he wants to hang himself with a silk scarf that is fragrant with the scent of the motorcycle girl, Sóla G—, that's just what he'll do.


Toward morning he dreams about the gentleman of the night before.

It seems to him that he is looking into a bedroom with rose-patterned wallpaper, velvet curtains, and a luxuriously made-up bed with plump pillows and a thick eiderdown. On the wall above the headboard hangs a painting in a gilt frame, depicting a gabled, turf-roofed farmhouse at the foot of a high mountain with four peaks, and a river in the foreground. To the boy it looks like the farm where he used to live with his mother until she died and he was sent away.

The man enters the room. He takes off his dressing gown, hangs it over the back of a chair, and climbs into the bed. Then he turns to the painting and runs his fingers along the gilt frame. At that the painting slides to one side, like a panel from a hatch, to reveal a secret compartment containing a casket the size of a beer crate. The man lifts this out of the cavity, places it on the bedside table, and opens it. Inside is a human head with curly red hair. The boy recognizes his own head.

The man lies down in bed, takes the boy's head out of the casket, and lays it on the pillow beside him, then draws up the quilt to its chin. The head's eyes open.

From the pillow the boy can see his body standing at the foot of the bed, dressed up in his Sunday best but lacking a head.

His head begins to laugh; the body shakes with laughter.

**II**

(October 19–20, 1918)

# iv

Reykjavík has two picture houses, the Old Cinema and the New Cinema. Films are shown daily at both, one or two on working days and three on Sundays. Each screening lasts from one to two and a half hours, though lately films have become so long that they sometimes have to be shown over consecutive evenings.

The boy watches all the movies that are imported to Iceland. As a rule, he goes to both cinemas on the same day and sees most films as often as he can.

He was eleven years old when he saw his first motion picture, in the autumn of 1913. On the first day of summer that year, Pastor Fridrik, public benefactor to the boys of the town, had founded within the YMCA movement a brigade modeled on foreign scout troops, called the Varangians after the Norse warriors who had once fought for the emperors of Byzantium. The old lady had got wind of this and, on the strength of her connection with the man of God—she'd shared a bed with Pastor Fridrik's maternal aunt for a whole winter when they were both young hired hands—pleaded with him to accept into the Varangian troop an unfortunate orphan whose upbringing had been dumped on her five years before.

She had, she said, no more idea than anyone else from the countryside how to bring up a child in town; the boy was an outsider and at the age when, if nothing were done, he would join the rabble of little savages who roamed Reykjavík's main street, squealing like pigs, chucking horse manure at passersby, and tipping over cyclists. Either that or—which she found more likely—he would end his days in the attic, since he was already such a loner that rather than go out and play with his classmates he preferred to hang around at home, smoking cigarettes with her.

The boy had overheard her saying something of the sort to Pastor Fridrik, since he had been ordered to wait outside in the passage, munching hard candies, while they had their talk.

Once the old lady had finished her piece, the boy was summoned into the office. Imposing youth leader and puny youngster looked one another in the eye. After they had studied each other for a while, Pastor Fridrik announced:

—He's a promising lad. I'll take him.

Then, stroking his distinguished beard, he added:

—But he'll have to stop smoking.

The business of being a Varangian turned out to be insufferably dull. The other youths knew the boy from school and shunned him just as they did there. It all boiled down to being a strapping young man and currying favor with the patrol leaders who led the brigade in the scout training that was intended to enhance their virility and mental powers. Most bearable for the boy were the occasions when they were permitted to dress up in the costume of the Varangian Guard, after the fashion of the men of old, in blue-and-white tunic, red cloak, and blue-and-red cap, both because he enjoyed making his cloak swirl around his thighs and because it allowed him to become somebody else.

Then, on the first day of winter, the proprietor of the Old Cinema invited the Varangians to attend the premiere of *The White Glove Band*, on condition that they turn up in their full regalia.

That night, for the first time that he could remember, the boy dreamed.

The Varangians made no further trips to the cinema, so he stopped attending. Instead, he made a pact with the old lady that providing he didn't take up smoking again, he would be allowed to go to the pictures.

And now the boy lives in the movies. When not spool-ing them into himself through his eyes, he is replaying them in his mind.

Sleeping, he dreams variations on the films, in which the web of incident is interwoven with strands from his own life.

But he has yet to dream of Sóla G—.

# V

The boy is loafing idly on the pavement outside Hotel Iceland. He has just emerged from the Chaplin film at the New Cinema and is waiting to go to the latest Fatty caper at nine o'clock on the other side of the square. Both the town's screens are showing nothing but riotous comedies, presumably because today a referendum is being held on the country's independence, and life is supposed to be fun. Not that the boy is affected by the fuss, as he has no more right to vote than anyone else under forty. Still, the clowning and slapstick of Fatty and Chaplin can be enjoyed at any age and can just as easily raise a laugh for the twenty-third time.

There's a convivial atmosphere around the hotel, as there always is when a passenger ship is in port. The steamer *Botnia* docked at coffee time, having voyaged from Copenhagen with a cargo of people and freight. Men and women of the better sort wander in and out of the lobby; strange languages hover in the air, mingling with the fragrant blue tobacco smoke from cigarettes and cigars; the town's followers of fashion are out in force to cast an eye over the foreign visitors' tailoring, and in the hotel dining room a brand-new gramophone record is playing. Interspersed with this modern feast for the senses is a cacophony of barking and neighing, creaking of harnesses, and shouts of "ho, ho, ho," while piles of dung, deposited by the horses of recent arrivals from over the mountains, steam gently in the cool evening air.

It would be incorrect to say that the boy is wholly idle as he loiters there on the hotel sidewalk. He is, in fact, amusing himself by analyzing the life around him, with an acuity honed by watching some five hundred films in which every glance, every movement, every expression, and every pose is charged with meaning and clues as to the subject's inner feelings and intentions, whether for good or for evil. Indeed, all mankind's behavior is an open book to him—how people conduct themselves in groups, large or small; their relationship to every conceivable thing; their movements in all kinds of interior, in the streets, in the town and country—since the simplified and exaggerated miming of the actors has made it easier for the boy to fix it all in his mind.

His attention is particularly drawn to a knot of young men who have gathered by the hotel doors. Although they are dressed up in their best suits to gain entrance to the dining room, he recognizes among them three former Varangians, who are now at the College for Marine Engineers. He overhears them saying that some of the *Botnia*'s crew are ill with the same influenza that ravaged the country last summer, and that the ship will be delayed while new hands are found to take their place. The boy knows the illness from personal experience. He was as sick as a dog for five days, with a headache and a high temperature, a cold and an upset stomach, and missed the films *From Headquarters* and *The Black Owl*, neither of which, to his great dismay, has been shown again.

One of the boys from the engineers' college shows his companions a ring he is wearing on the little finger of his left hand: a silver ring with a black stone. It is a gift from his sister, who has today returned from Denmark after six months' training in home economics at the *smørrebrød* school in Odense. The youth holds up the ring to catch the glow of the gaslight by the hotel entrance, and his friends duly admire it. He kisses the black stone: Sis really is the best! What a pity she couldn't come along this evening, but she's feeling a bit out of sorts after the voyage.

The cathedral bell tolls nine.

The group of friends is drawn into Hotel Iceland.

The boy dashes across the square: the projectionist at the Old Cinema is as punctual as the sun.

# vi

—Moonstone . . .

The boy makes a puzzled sound. The man points at him:

—*Your name, Máni Steinn, Moonstone . . .*

He repeats the word, mimicking the man's pronunciation:

—Mún-stón . . .

The man nods gravely.

—*Yes, you are . . .*

The boy translates the words in his head: "Yes, you are." Is English such a simple language, then, that it fits Icelandic word for word? Perhaps he could learn it like that, beginning with the words that are exactly the same, if he repeats them often enough?

He points at the man.

—Yú neim . . .

The man laughs.

—*Is none of your business . . .*

Turning serious again, he runs his fingers through the boy's dark-red hair.

—*Auburn moon, harvest moon . . .*

This requires more effort in language learning than the boy can be bothered to make. Yet, unable to resist the temptation, he repeats:

—Óborn mún, nonn off yor bisniss . . .

Smiling at the man, he seizes his hand and removes it from his head to place it between his legs. They are under the covers in the man's bed in Hotel Iceland.

The man turns away from the boy, pressing against his hot body and guiding the boy's hard member inside himself.

◆

*Spring turns to Autumn over night*
*In Flanders field,*
*Before its time the corn is cut,*
*Your auburn hair,*
*A harvest meal by ravens pluck'd.*
                    —From *Billy* by Anonymous (1915)

◆

After the Fatty short was over, the boy had wandered around the center of town, ending up by the illuminated window of Café Skjaldbreid.

A foreigner was sitting at a table inside, reading a book through a pair of pince-nez. He was about thirty, and the boy was intrigued by his fair waxed mustache and wavy hair. After a few minutes, the man sensed that he was being watched. Lowering his book, he glanced around. When finally he caught sight of the boy's face in the window, he turned chalk-white and leaped to his feet.

The boy waited for him outside in the dark street, his back to the café, and let the man come right up to him before he turned. The man held out a shaking hand as if he couldn't believe the boy was of this world.

—Billy?


After the boy had crawled in through the window of his hotel room and they had begun to take off their clothes, the man unfastened the artificial leg made of hardwood that was attached with a leather harness to his right thigh.

The boy had never seen such a device before and examined the leg from every angle until the man took it away from him and hung it from the foot of the bed. He drew Máni Steinn under the covers to join him:

—*Moonstone* . . .

**III**

(October 31–November 1, 1918)

# vii

Almost all anyone in Reykjavík can talk about these days is the "Spanish flu," which, it is now believed, was carried to the country on the steamship *Botnia*.

Cables from Copenhagen report that the pestilence is raging there with devastating virulence; comparisons are being made with the cholera epidemic that ravaged the city in 1853. At the same time, articles appear in the Reykjavík papers with statements by respected Danish physicians claiming that the symptoms of the disease are no more serious than might be expected from common influenza, and that there is no cause to resort to drastic and costly preventative measures, since the mortality rate must be regarded as within acceptable limits. Endorsing this policy, the Icelandic Board of Health merely urges the public to take precautions similar to those they would take for the seasonal grippe that does the rounds every year. Other voices are heard saying that no notice should be taken of the bleating of the Dane, since he is made of different stuff from the

Icelanders—those proud descendants of the Viking warrior Egill Skallagrímsson.

But with every day that passes without government action, more of the townspeople are struck down with symptoms just like those described in the news from Denmark as afflicting the lesser race. These include painful pneumonia, physical prostration, nervous depression, and fever.

The boy has heard the old lady reading these things aloud to herself from copies of *Morgunbladid*, which she receives gratis at the end of every week when their landlord downstairs has finished with them. For such skill had she brought to wiping this man's bottom in his infancy that, once her working days were over, he had invited her to live in his attic rent-free. Later, when she was asked to take in the boy, the landlord had made no objection to his living with her. And this despite the fact the blessed man is a *socialist*—and all his folk, as the old lady exclaims every time the family downstairs does her a kindness.

The boy has learned in addition that at number 5 Raudarárstígur there is a used cooking stove for sale; that Mrs. Harlyk is to lead a meeting of the Salvation Army; that a marriage has taken place between the painter Fridrik E. Borgfjörd and Ólöf Bjarnadóttir of Lambastadir; that such Danish foodstuffs as *appetitsild*, *ansjoser*, and *sardiner* are available from Einar Árnason's stores; that a purse has been lost and a silver brooch found, because the old lady enunciates every last word that is printed in the papers.

He is grateful for the old lady's noisy delight in reading; were it not for her, he wouldn't know the first thing about home or world affairs, since he himself is so illiterate—the letters of the alphabet disguise themselves before his eyes, glide between lines, switch roles in the middle of a word, and might as well be a red code to which he does not have the key—that he can barely struggle through the programs and title cards at the cinema.

Although, as a rule, little in the papers captures his interest—anything that happens in Iceland seems too small, while overseas events affect him only if they are grand enough to be made into films—the news in the last few days about the Spanish flu has held a lurid fascination for the boy:

He has a butterfly in his stomach, similar to those he experiences when he picks up a gentleman, only this time it is larger, its wingspan greater, its color as black as the velvet ribbons on a hearse.

An uncontrollable force has been unleashed in the country; something historic is taking place in Reykjavík at the same time as it is happening in the outside world.

The silver screen has torn and a draft is blowing between the worlds.

"But where is Sóla G—?"

The boy has not seen her for nineteen days, not since that night on Öskjuhlíð.

# viii

The fires of Katla are dying down, but the plume of ash can still be glimpsed on the horizon when the cloud cover permits. This morning the citizens of Reykjavík awoke to find a layer of ash covering their windowpanes. At ten o'clock it was still so dark in the bedrooms of the town that one would have thought it was the middle of the night. Many have risen late as a result, and people are still coming to terms with reality when the boy gets up at midday.

He performs his habitual circuit of the town, checking which films are to be shown that evening—*The Spoilers* at the New Cinema, *Hearts in Exile* at the Old—then buys himself some curds at the Fjallkonan restaurant and peruses the picture papers at S. Jón's Bookshop. But today this is merely a pretext.

The boy invariably arranges his route so it passes the house belonging to the parents of Sóla G——. There is no movement inside. He is relieved. She cannot be lying ill indoors.

It begins to rain. The ash runs in gray streams down the walls, cascading into the street. It is sticky underfoot.

—Were you giving me the eye at the bathhouse yesterday?

 —So what if I was?

 —I thought maybe you wanted me to drop by.

 —Maybe I did.

 —Well, here I am.

The boy is standing in the yard behind the Á.C. photographic studio. The rain rattles on the corrugated-iron porch over the back entrance. The photographer leans against the doorpost, studying the boy, then says curtly:

 —Come in.

Unusually, the photographer does not attempt to kiss him but only wants them to jerk each other off. They are quick to come. The photographer hands the boy three krónur:

 —I'm afraid you won't be as busy for a while, pal.

The boy shrugs and heads back out into the rain.

The photographer was one of his first gentlemen. It was from him that he acquired the photograph of Muggur. The picture shows the artist in a black suit, with bangs down to his eyes and a roguish smile on his lips. There is a cigarette in his hand, which he must have lowered the instant the shutter opened.

The movement of his arm is sketched in the air as if Muggur had made a brushstroke in time.

The boy's next stop is the yard of the Reykjavík Automobile Association, where Sóla G— is permitted to tinker with her motorcycle in return for helping to clean the taxicabs. He hovers at a discreet distance from the workshop, watching the vehicles come and go. The drivers are used to lads hanging around and pay no attention to the boy, apart from one who winks at him. The boy ignores this but makes a mental note of the man's face together with the noise of his engine.

The girl is not there and does not show her face during the hour or more that the boy waits.

Darkness begins to fall once more. The town ambulance speeds in the direction of Sudurgata. Beside the driver, a young woman in a wide-brimmed hat sits staring palely ahead.

The boy sets off home. He must eat his dinner so he can carry on his search for the girl.

He whistles a tune as he walks and smiles when he realizes where he heard it. The sound had wafted down from the upper floor into the storeroom of the photographic studio.

The names Peter and Pan float along with the melody.

Before Máni Steinn discovered Sóla G—, he had thought Muggur the fairest of them all.

# ix

When the boy next sees Sóla G— she is among a gaggle of girls outside a house in Vonarstræti where dressmaking is taught and, it is rumored, women's rights are discussed.

In this company she is dressed, like any other Reykjavík society girl, according to the latest fashion, in an English lady's trench coat, a knitted hat in green and brown, and buttoned leather boots that disappear under the hem of her calf-length skirt. Compared with her motorcycle outfit, the boy has to admit this getup is disappointingly conventional.

But it's all right. He knows that it's in the nature of women like Sóla G— and Irma Vep, her French doppelgänger played by Musidora in *The Vampires*, to don a thousand disguises and be simultaneously "Everywoman" and "The One Woman"—even when dressed in suit and tie.

◆

*The Vampires* (*Les Vampires*) is a seven-hour-long French film by Louis Feuillade. Over ten episodes it tells the story of the eponymous gang of nihilists who hold French society in the grip of fear. Under the leadership of their brilliant and ruthless master, the Grand Vampire, they have penetrated the highest echelons of society, corrupting everyone they can, intimidating and murdering all those they cannot.

Paris is in disarray, unpredictable and lethal. People are murdered in cafés and railway carriages, in the streets, in back rooms, and in their own bedrooms. Every other person is in disguise, name and social rank are no guarantee—the haute bourgeoisie cannot distinguish their own from members of the criminal gang—every pocket conceals a weapon, every closet a corpse; new mechanical inventions are used to commit elaborate crimes. In a city where reason is daily executed with its own weapons, nowhere is safe.

Foremost among the Vampires is the girl Irma Vep. Wearing a black costume that clings to the curves of her shapely figure, she scales buildings like a shadow and breaks into apartments and government offices before making her escape over the rooftops.

And all is achieved with the cheerful zeal of one who has turned her back on the laws of her fellow men.

O Irma Vep, queen of the cloud-veiled night!

The dressmaking group prepares to head home, with all the hugging and kissing that invariably attend womankind. The girls who live in the "gods," the neighborhood of streets named for the old Norse pantheon, are to walk together south around the lake and up the hill; two of the others are going to cycle along the shore to the west end of town; while the rest plan to stroll arm in arm down to Lækjartorg Square to promenade a little before heading up Hverfisgata and home. But these plans are cut short when the sewing mistress appears on the steps and calls them over.

The girls turn cheerful faces toward her, but the woman's grave expression soon spreads to their own. They hurry over and she beckons them back inside.

Sóla G— is last to mount the steps. It seems to the boy that just as the door is closing behind her, her glance falls on his hiding place.

◆

There is only one topic of conversation at the New Cinema box office:

The youth from the engineers' college infected by his sister—the *smørrebrød* lady who arrived with the *Botnia*—has died of the sickness.

# IV

(November 5–6, 1918)

# X

In the five days that have passed since the first influenza fatality, the cinemas have become ever quieter, yet the townspeople have stubbornly continued to attend. Especially the young, whose response to the fear of contagion is to cluster together while the adults stay at home. Besides, it is warmer in the cinemas than in most of their homes, now that the coal shortage and the high price of paraffin have begun to bite, and coziest of all packed into the seats farthest from the auditorium doors.

But as the flu takes its toll on the musicians—not only those whose livelihood it is to accompany the films but also the ones immediately recruited to fill their places on an assortment of the unlikeliest instruments—the silence grows.

By the time Miss Inga María Waagfjörd, guitar player and chanteuse, slumps unconscious from the piano stool during the second episode of *The Golden Reel* at the New Cinema, the epidemic has snatched away the last person in Reykjavík capable of picking out a tune.

The following evening there is an attempt at the Old Cinema to screen the Italian smuggling tale *Anger* without any musical accompaniment. It is a disaster.

It takes less than half an hour for the audience to lose interest in the events on screen. When the only sounds accompanying the pictures are the coughing and throat-clearing supplied by the cinemagoers themselves, together with those emanating from the projectionist's booth—the growling of the motor that powers the projector and the whispering of the film as it unwinds from the top reel, is pulled through the light beam, and threads onto the lower with a slightly hoarser whisper—it becomes apparent just how silent these films really are.

The actors' movements seem clumsy, the pace too slow for the melodramatic plot, and the cuts between scenes confusing. It makes no difference how brilliantly the great diva Francesca Bertini performs the role of Elena the mountain maid in this third installment of *The Seven Deadly Sins*, which she both produces and stars in—she cannot hold the audience's attention; it would take more than that to compete with the silence and the reality beyond the timber walls.

In the quiet gloom, beneath the hissing, flickering light, members of the audience begin to murmur about the situation in the town. In an undertone at first, but soon at normal pitch. Others join in, and before long the screening has turned into a public meeting at which stories are swapped about the nature of the epidemic.

All are agreed that the information supplied by the surgeon general fails to convey the truth about the terrible symptoms of the disease, which are quite unlike any the townspeople have experienced before. The body temperature soars so fast, for example, that by the first or second day the patient is helpless with delirium—and then there is the bleeding.

The projectionist's silhouette appears in the aperture.

The projector beam is switched off.

Lights come on in the wall lamps.

The young people glance around, and only now does it dawn on them how many members of the audience have been taken ill: every other face is chalk-white; lips are blue, foreheads glazed with sweat, nostrils red, eyes sunken and wet.

Silence falls on the gathering.

Moving cautiously, the cinemagoers begin to ease themselves out of the rows of seats, pick their way up the aisle, and vanish noiselessly from the hall.

The final picture show is over.

The boy had already left some time before.

# xi

Reykjavík has undergone a transformation.

An ominous hush lies over the busiest, most bustling part of town. No hoofbeats, no rattling of cart wheels or rumble of automobiles, no roar of motorcycles or ringing of bicycle bells. No rasp of sawing from the carpenters' workshops, or clanging from the forges, or slamming of warehouse doors. No gossiping voices of washerwomen on their way to the hot springs, no shouts of dockworkers unloading the ships, or cries of newspaper hawkers on the main street. No smell of fresh bread from the bakeries, or waft of roasting meat from the restaurants.

The doors of the shops neither open nor close—no one goes in, no one comes out—no one hurries home from work or goes to work at all.

No one says good morning. No one says good night.

The cathedral bell doesn't toll the quarter hour, or even the hours themselves. Though the hands stand at eight minutes past three, it's hard to guess whether this refers to day or night. A gloomy pall of cloud shrouds both sun and moon. A deathly quiet reigns in the afternoon as if it were the darkest hour before dawn. Or not quite . . .

From the long, low shed by the harbor the sounds of banging and planing can be heard, though each hammer blow and bout of sawing is so muffled and muted to the ear that it seems almost to apologize for disturbing the silence. It is here that the coffins are being made.

Four more have died of the influenza: a thirty-five-year-old grocer, a girl in her teens, a woman of twenty-eight and the child she was carrying. And a third of the townspeople have taken to their beds, gravely ill.

By the end of the working day the undertaker has received five new orders for coffins—and two more will await him at home.

The streets yawn, empty of people, except for glimpses here and there of the odd shadowy figure out and about. These are the old women, bundled up in black clothes, wearing shawl upon shawl to keep out the chill. They have given room to so many ailments in their day that the scourge now making a meal of their descendants can find no morsel worth having on their worn-out old bones.

If word gets around that someone has a drop of lamp oil, cough syrup, or vinegar to spare; if it is rumored that oats, rice, soap, or dried stewing vegetables will be sold at the Thomsen's Magasin warehouse door for half an hour at eleven; if news spreads that a packet of salt fish failed to make it onto the ship or a sack containing a handful of sprouting potatoes has been left sitting around open and unattended, an old biddy will layer up in skirt upon skirt and two pairs of mittens, and hobble off into town for the sake of posterity.

They come face-to-face in courtyards, side streets, alleyways, and gardens—stooping figures—acknowledging one another with sidelong glances and twitching lips.

The boy is also on the prowl in the deserted center of town.

He'd had no inkling that when the pestilence took hold Reykjavík would empty and convey the impression that nothing was happening at all; that the town would become an abandoned set that he, Máni Steinn, could envisage as the backdrop for whatever sensational plot he cared to devise, or, more accurately, for the kind of sinister events that in a film would be staged in this sort of village of the damned—for these days the real stories are being acted out behind closed doors. And they are darker than a youthful mind can begin to imagine.

The boy pauses.

A cry is heard from the undertaker's house.

# xii

The old lady's attic has little in the way of heating. Owing to the shortage of coal, she's fallen back on two paraffin stoves that she doesn't dare to leave burning at night for fear of fire. A faint warmth filters up from the floors below, but it's much feebler than the heat she's used to receiving secondhand from the landlord and his household over the winter months—for the socialist and other important folk are feeling the pinch too—no one can be found to stoke their boiler any longer.

To combat the cold the old lady spends her days in bed, kitted out in balaclava and mittens, under a heap of eiderdowns, blankets, and overcoats that she gets the boy to pile over her before he leaves the house. There she lies right around the clock, reading the papers by day, dozing by night, rising only to cook the boy his porridge in the mornings and his fish tail and potatoes at night, to wring out his clothes and her own, to iron and darn, mop the damp from the floors and walls, and puff her way through thirty cigarettes.

And since the young mistress and her elder daughter fell ill, the old lady has been popping downstairs to cook for the landlord and his younger children; to nurse the patients, wash their clothes, and boil their compresses and rags.

Never in all her born days can the old lady recall spending so much time lounging around in bed.

There's the boy now, climbing the ladder to the attic.

A sequence that he has been trying to shake off for the last hour keeps repeating itself over and over in his mind:

A horse-drawn carriage careers at breakneck speed down the slope of Bakarabrekka, over the bridge, and into Lækjartorg Square. The dwarfish driver is bound to the box with a broad leather strap. His head is encased in a black turban, the long end muffling his face; his gleaming black eyes flick to and fro beneath immensely bushy brows. He brandishes his whip like a madman, raining down the lash on the horses' flanks, and they stretch out their necks at a gallop, snorting till they foam at the bits.

On the roof of the carriage stands a female figure in a long cloak that flaps in the wind like a huge bat spreading its wings. With the razor-sharp, nine-inch claws on her half-human hands, the creature rips open the carriage roof, sending splinters of wood flying like hail into the louring black night.

Two men are sitting inside, one young, the other older. Overcome with terror, the older man cowers against the younger.

The boy appears in the opening at the top of the ladder.

Only once he has emerged onto the landing does he mentally pause the footage, freezing it on a tight frame of the older man's fleshy hand clutching at the younger man's thigh. The thick fingers dig into the pale-colored trouser material, the middle one sporting a gold ring embellished with a large gem.

The boy looks across the attic.

A candle is burning on the stool beside the old lady's bed: she's awake, then.

Becoming aware of him, she sits up.

The boy freezes in his tracks.

Before his eyes, sixty years fall away from the old lady. Her features are softened by the yellow glow of the guttering flame and the rust-brown balaclava frames them like a loose fall of hair.

She takes on the appearance of a woman the boy has not seen for many a long year, becoming the living image of her youngest sister's granddaughter.

The boy sinks to the floor with a groan.

—Mother . . .

# V

(November 6–11, 1918)

# xiii

The stairway up to the projectionist's booth is like a shaft supplying oxygen to a blazing furnace.

The boy clings to the rail, struggling to resist the force that is sucking him inexorably closer. He leans back until he is almost horizontal, bracing his feet against the steps as if the world is standing on end and he is fighting to climb backward up the stairs that lead straight down into the fiery mouth of the oven.

It crosses his mind that it would be easier to crawl away than to reverse, but when he turns he is hit head-on by the blast, loses his grip on the rail, and is flung with colossal force up the steps and in through the door of the projectionist's booth.

The booth is filled with an ear-splitting noise and a searing inferno.

The projector is as big as a horse, its reels like wagon wheels, the car engine that drives it glowing red with the strain. The lamp is as dazzling as the sun; blinding light shines out of every chink in the machine.

The projectionist is pacing around the booth, striking his clenched fist into his palm. He is drenched with sweat, which sprays from him at every turn he takes. From where the boy is lying in a huddle by the door, he can see the drops sizzling on the scalding metal, evaporating and leaving behind tiny rings of salt.

The boy himself is burning up. He opens his mouth in the hope that some of the sweat will find its way inside.

The man stops dead when he notices the gaping boy. He points at the wall in front of the projector. The wall is intact where the opening for the light-beam should be. The picture projected onto it is no bigger than a postcard.

When the boy doesn't react, the man raises him to his feet, leads him in front of the thundering machine, and stations him so the film is projected onto his chest.

The heat close to the machine is even more suffocating than over by the door, and the boy chokes as he breathes in the blistering air.

He begins to cough.


The film on his chest shows a close-up of gas blowing out of a heating vent in an opulently papered wall. Cut to smartly dressed guests in a ballroom. Close-up of the gas smoking out of the vent on his breastbone. Cut to men and women running around in confusion.

Close-up of the smoking gas. Cut to the guests beating on the locked doors. Close-up of the gas. Cut to the guests trying to break into the boy's lungs. Close-up of the gas. Cut to the guests lying comatose. Cut to black-clad criminals in gas masks, who steal into the ballroom, out from between the boy's ribs.

The more the boy coughs, the hotter he becomes.

The projectionist shouts to him over the thundering of the engine, then begins to strip off his clothes. When he has removed every last stitch apart from a green woolen kneesock on his right leg, the lights go on in the gymnasium adjoining the booth. A rock the height of a man, made of moon-pale stone, stands in the middle of the floor.

The projectionist waves to the boy and bounds into the gym. Giving the rock a measuring look, he limbers up, stretches, flexes his biceps, sizes up the rock again, then heaves it over his head and tosses it some ten yards with ease. Then, strolling after it, he repeats the trick again and again.

This is accompanied by tremendous crashes.

The coughing boy gets a hard-on.

# xiv

The boy is standing in the doorway of a storeroom.

A human figure, swathed in black from head to foot, is leaning against a large wooden box. Around its waist is a black chain that falls heavily over its loins. The box comes up to the figure's middle. Beneath the hem of its skirt the toe of a shoe peeps out.

—A little closer, dear, a little closer . . .

The tinny voice emanating from inside the box sounds like a scratched gramophone record.

—A little closer, dear, a little closer . . .

The floorboards glisten. Ropes of gray slime stretch out like the filaments of a net from the toe under the skirt across the room to the boy's bare feet.

—A little closer, dear, a little closer . . .

The black garment billows—something is moving inside, from the hips up the body to the head and back down the same way—until the figure thrusts two clenched, gloved fists out through the slits in the middle.

—A little closer, dear, a little closer . . .

The gloved fists open. Each contains a handful of flesh: cheeks, firm and ruddy, with smooth skin and a hint of dimples. It seems to the boy as if they have been ripped from his own face.

—A little closer, dear, a little closer . . .

The cheeks are slapped down, side by side, on the lid of the box.

—A little closer, dear, a little closer . . .

The hands disappear inside the slits. The garment billows.

—A little closer, dear, a little closer . . .

The toe of the shoe is thrust out from beneath the skirt and stamped down with such force that the floor creaks. Gray slime wells up between the boards. The air grows thick with the stench of rotting fish.

—A little closer, dear, a little closer . . .

The hands reappear. The figure flings a pair of eyebrows onto the lid. Pain lacerates the boy. He raises a hand to his forehead, but it is shaking too much for him to feel whether his own brows are still there.

—A little closer, dear, a little closer . . .

The figure withdraws its hands inside its clothes.

—A little closer, dear, a little closer . . .

The gramophone voice buzzes inside the wooden box.

—A little closer, dear, a little closer . . .

The veiled figure bangs down a nose between the cheeks and a moving mouth below it. The floorboards creak. The slime flows over the boy's feet.

Green eyes are cast onto the lid of the box. And a chin.

—A little closer, dear, a little closer . . .

A handful of teeth.

—A little closer, dear, a little closer . . .

A fistful of red locks.

—A little closer, dear . . .

The gramophone slows its revolutions. The voice drawls.

—A little . . .

The black garment billows around the figure. It holds out its gloved hands, a woman's breast resting in each.

—Closer . . .

The boy cries out. At last he knows what is expected of him. But he's too late. He's rooted to the spot.

—Closer . . .

He sucks up the gray slime through his bare soles.

—Closer . . .

Milk oozes from the nipples.

# XV

Plashing waves. Summer-pink light. The tide is going out. Small, twinkling-footed birds are busy pecking for insects at the water's edge. He is standing in a bed of tansy where the beach shelves down, taking care not to frighten them. The sunlight sparkles on the waves, which foam dark red at the crests as they roll over themselves.

◆

The boy examines himself in a hand mirror, spreading the dark blood on his lips with the tip of his tongue. Blood spurts from the corners of both his eyes, runs along the lids, and stays there like lines drawn by a master's hand. Ropes of blood pour from his nostrils to form a thick mustache. Drops of blood congeal on his earlobes.

◆

Hearing someone calling his name, he looks away from the shorebirds, whose movements are hampered now by having to wade through the thickening blood. By the three-story building that stands on the spit, a big wash is under way in huge tubs. The water steams. He hurries over to the washerwomen. The blood dyes the birds up to their breast feathers.

◆

The nails of the boy's left hand put on a spurt of growth, becoming as long as fingers in the blink of an eye. Both fingers and hand triple in size all at once, with a cracking of the bones. He drops the mirror. His shadow is lying on the floor, stubbornly human in shape. The shadow stretches its limbs and leaps to its feet, distorting the boy.

◆

"Tut, tut," say the washerwomen when he reaches them. "Tut, tut, look how he's dirtied himself!" They chivy him out of his clothes and sling him into the boiling water with the bloodied bedclothes. Push him to and fro with the laundry bats, pound him, lift him out and dunk him down again, until he's as soft as linen.

◆

The boy no longer has any need of blood or bone, muscle or gut. He dissolves his body, turning solid into liquid, beginning from within and rinsing it all out, until it gushes out of every orifice he can find. He is a shadow that passes from man to man, and no one is complete until he has cast him.

◆

He is hoisted out of the tub, flung onto the wringer, and thoroughly squeezed dry; then two washerwomen take him by the arms and legs, stretch him between them, and hang him out with the rest of the laundry. "I reckon it should fit her now," he hears the larger woman say as they walk away from the line.

◆

In the evening, when the birds on the shore have drowned in the boy's blood, Sóla G— comes and fetches Máni Steinn from the washing line. She takes him home and puts him on. She thinks his red lips, lined eyes, and earrings suit her, but she washes off his mustache and sheathes his nails.

# VI

(November 11–17, 1918)

# XVI

—This one's not dead.

—But he isn't breathing . . .

—He *is* breathing, faintly.

—But he hasn't got a pulse . . .

—If he's breathing, his heart must be beating.

Half-awake, the boy feels a metal object being placed against his left breast and held there.

The old lady's voice:

—But his hands are like ice . . .

The unknown man's voice shushes her brusquely.

A moment's silence.

—His heartbeat's regular. He's alive.

The metal object is removed from the boy's chest. His undershirt is buttoned up. The quilt is drawn over him again.

The old lady:

—Aren't you going to take him, then?

The man:

—There's no need. How are you yourself keeping, ma'am?

Her:

—I'm alive too.

Him:

—So I'd noticed.

The boy manages to crack open an eye.

—I owe it all to these . . .

The old lady's gnarl-veined hand intrudes into the boy's narrow field of vision, holding a sea-green packet of Three Castles cigarettes.

—Surely not.

The man, who is sitting on the edge of the boy's bed, shifts position. It is Dr. Garibaldi Árnason, the surgeon.

—You couldn't spare one?

The boy half opens his eyes. The doctor reaches out a hand and extracts a cigarette from the packet. The old lady sticks a match in the paraffin stove and gives him a light.

He draws the smoke deep into his lungs. She watches him smoke the cigarette halfway down.

—How is the landlord's family doing? They haven't wanted me downstairs since the boy was taken poorly.

—The son's with us at the French Hospital; he hasn't got long to live. The daughter's not quite as bad.

The old lady:

—Hell and damnation . . .

She breaks off, then adds:

—God bless the landlord and all his *socialist* folk.

The doctor pats the quilt.

—One's grateful for every life that's saved.

He rises to his feet.

—And, thanks to you, this fellow's going to pull through.

The boy blinks. The doctor turns away from the bed and addresses someone at the other end of the attic:

—Would you get the car ready, please?

The boy raises his head from the pillow.

On the landing stands a figure with hypnotic eyes.

Sóla G— gives the boy a conspiratorial smile—gestures to her neck and from there to the red scarf that is knotted around Máni Steinn's own—then lowers herself nimbly through the stair opening.

As the boy is drifting off again, he hears the old lady pestering the doctor to take the packet of cigarettes in return for his help; his need is greater than hers.

Dr. Garibaldi replies that it is more important she herself stays fit and sees to it that as soon as the boy is back on his feet he presents himself at the emergency hospital in the Midtown School, where they could use some stout lads.

# xvii

The morning the boy was up and about again it was officially announced in Paris that an armistice had been signed between the Allies and the Germans. According to the handbills circulating the news, the announcement was accompanied by a salvo of gunfire and scenes of wild jubilation.

In Reykjavík the cessation of hostilities was greeted with the same indifference as the cessation of the Katla eruption a few days before. And indeed the sight that confronts the boy's eyes when he arrives in the yard of the Midtown School resembles nothing so much as scenes from a field hospital in a Pathé newsreel. There has been no cease-fire in the influenza's war on the inhabitants of the town.

The school is simultaneously orphanage and hospital, lunatic asylum and mortuary. Charabancs and horse-drawn carts come and go in a constant stream: bringing in critically ill patients for admission and cure;

carrying away corpses to the cemetery chapel to be laid in coffins and buried.

All is performed with well-oiled efficiency, so swiftly has necessity taught people to service the sick and the dead.


The boy hasn't set foot on the school grounds since he left at age twelve, at the bottom of his class.

Before he knows it, he is standing at the foot of the high wall along Laufásvegur, in the "invisible spot" that used to be his refuge during break, where he could watch his fellow pupils from a safe distance—for it had dawned on him that the choice was his; that it was he who declined to take part in the other children's games before they had a chance to leave him out. The day has yet to come when he will voluntarily mingle with his contemporaries.

Now here he is, back in his old lookout, and despite the appalling state of affairs, he is, as he was then, un-moved by the scenes unfolding before his eyes.


—Are you just going to stand there like a spare part, boy?

Three men are waiting beside a boxlike stretcher that is sticking halfway off the back of a truck. They are short a fourth man to support the foot end on the left-hand side. With them is a nurse, and it is she who calls to ask if the boy is going to make himself useful.

The yellow box would look just like a coffin were it not for the window in the lid, which admits light and air, and allows the invalid to see out. Ashen-gray fingers with purple nails grope at the edge of this opening, as tentatively as the petals of a small flower awakening, and suddenly a delicate hand emerges onto the lid. The white lace at the wrist is stiff with blood.

Next thing he knows, the boy is shouldering the box with the other three men, and they are carrying it in through the main entrance of the school.

On the way to the emergency room, the boy notices that the assembly hall and all the classrooms on the ground floor have been converted into hospital wards. Every bed contains a patient far gone with the disease. Groans of suffering and anguish, and the sounds of adults and children weeping, can be heard out in the corridor. There are gas rings for heating water on tables here and there, and steam rises from large cauldrons.

In the classroom where the boy had failed to learn to read, they hold the box steady so the latest victim can be lifted onto the examination table. The nurse and a young doctor remove the lid. And the boy discovers that inside is the elder sister of one of his former classmates.

Her face is blotchy; her eyes are glazed.

By giving the boy a hard stare, the nurse manages to drag his attention away from the corpse. She points to a basin containing bloodstained sheets:

—Take this to the laundry, dear; then come back up here and I'll tell you what to do next.

# xviii

*The Angel of Death has entered among us with the great epidemic and cast a pall of the deepest despair over many of our homes.*

*Men and women of all ages and stations have been snatched away. Death makes no distinction, and one often feels that it strikes where it least should. It is beyond comprehension that parents should be carried off from their children, or that the elderly, with one foot in the grave, should be deprived of their sole support. If only people could be brought to a better understanding of their duties toward others beside themselves, then death's choice, which appears to us so harsh and unjust, would not be so impossible to understand. If only loving-kindness were a more potent force among us, a new provider and a new friend would come forward for all those who are bereft. And if only the devastating wave of grief could induce people to make more effort to bear goodwill to all men and show greater love and charity than before, it would not have broken over us in vain.*

*The great upsurge in loving-kindness that has been experienced around the world as a result of the late hostilities has barely touched us here. Will it not then occur to all those who believe in Divine Providence to wonder whether this terrible scourge has been released upon our nation expressly to awaken among us the same sentiment? Could any exhortation to give more thought to eternity be more memorable than that which our community has lately received?*

*Most of those who have crossed over to the other side were in their prime and had service yet to perform for the public good, however different they were in outward appearance. Most had friends and relatives who now bear a heavy burden of grief; parents bowed with age weep for their dashed hopes; those left alone in the world for their mainstay; children for their loving parents.*

*But happy in their grief are all those who, through their faith, are certain of a life hereafter. They know that this is but a brief parting, and that those who are gone have merely attained a higher plane of existence and have not vanished forever into dark graves.*

Below these words of consolation in *Morgunbladid* are printed the names of the eighty-two townsmen and -women who had died by the time the paper went to press on the eve of November 17.

The boy glances around the classroom, which is used as a rest area for the volunteers. His fellow workers are exhausted from the day's labors; no one is paying him any attention.

He folds the newspaper and tucks it inside his clothes, thinking it looks like something the old lady would enjoy.

Above the text there is a cross, bordered in black.

As the cinemas are still closed, he heads for home.

But first he is going to pay a visit to the National Library on Arnarhóll.

The basement is the refuge of Sívert Thordal, D.Phil., a stooping, downy-haired manuscript scholar. One would be forgiven for thinking that he was hiding away down there from the pestilence, but in fact, ever since the large white edifice was built, he has been allowed to dwell in a cubbyhole in its depths—for he is married to his research—and so Dr. Thordal always speaks of himself as the peculiar Atlas "of the Icelandic literary world, whose bowed spine bends but does not break beneath the weight of its heritage."

The boy sometimes allows this genial hunchback to suck him off for two krónur.

◆

He quickens his pace. He must get to bed in good time; he needs to be well rested for tomorrow's exertions.

The situation is now so desperate that there is barely anyone left in most homes with the strength to help the doctors' drivers to carry the worst cases. So a strapping fellow is to be assigned to every vehicle to assist them.

Máni Steinn has shown that he has what it takes.

Tomorrow morning he is to commence home visits with Dr. Garibaldi Árnason and his driver.

Dr. Garibaldi's driver is Sóla G—.

# VII

(November 25–26, 1918)

# xix

From morning to evening, from evening to night and through to the early hours, for nine days running, the boy accompanies Dr. Garibaldi Árnason and Sóla G— on visits to the sick.

They do the rounds in a vehicle borrowed from the Reykjavík Automobile Association, which the boy recognized immediately from the engine sound as belonging to the man who had winked at him in the garage yard. The man had died early that month, and when no driver was left at the station to take his place in the Ford, Sóla G— was called in and put behind the wheel, though she had no license: her skill at riding the red Indian was well known, and it did no harm either that Dr. Garibaldi had been at school with her father.

Every day the boy presents himself at the garage, where Sóla G— awaits him with a full tank and the engine growling in the gray dawn. They pick up the doctor, and then their first port of call is the health station, where Dr. Garibaldi fetches the list of the day's home visits, arranged according to the severity of the emergency.

The symptoms of the Spanish flu are as follows:

A raging fever (rising to 109), headache, earache, soreness in the throat and chest; a dry cough producing slimy mucus, either yellow or streaked with blood; pains in the muscles and joints; and diarrhea. Nosebleeds are common, especially among adolescents, and almost impossible to stanch. The blood gushes not only from the nostrils but from the ears and gums as well, coming up from the lungs and stomach, or down from the intestines and out through the urethra. And on top of this, the most lethal complications of all: acute bronchitis and pneumonia, even when people have made every effort to take care and stay in their beds.

The majority of the afflicted lie in a daze; the rest are unable to sleep. Men can run amok in their delirium—a danger to themselves and other members of their household—and cannot be restrained by any means other than an injection of scopolamine. All pregnant women fall ill and many go on to miscarry.

Often, once the pneumonia has abated and the fever has dropped, or even gone away altogether, the heart begins to race, and in no time at all the victim is finished off by a cardiac arrest, or else the face and limbs swell up and death comes about by suffocation.

In many cases the skin takes on a bluish tinge. Corpses turn blue-black.

There are ten thousand stricken townspeople, ten doctors, three overflowing hospitals, and one pharmacy, which is closed due to the illness of the druggist and all his dispensers.

All over town flu victims lie in a huddle, racked by coughs, aches, and dehydration, too delirious to fetch water to quench their thirst; in the more affluent homes, the medicine bottles stand within reach, untouched.

In one turf-roofed farmhouse on Brádrædisholt, in the west of town, they find the stiffened body of a man lying in the marital bed, and beside it a desperately ill woman with the corpse of an infant in the crook of each arm. Along the walls are cots, each with one or two heads peeping over the sides. The husband had died leaving five young children, and his wife had fallen ill before she could raise the alarm. Shortly afterward she gave birth to stillborn twins. A neighbor came upon her by chance.

While Dr. Garibaldi tends to the mother, Sóla and Máni shroud the bodies of the twins in pillowcases and carry them out to the car.

An hour later, on Grettisgata, they hear the death rattle of the solitary occupant at the very instant they enter the damp little basement room.

•

No matter how distressing the scenes, the boy remains impassive. Scarcely a word falls from his lips over the nine days.

Reykjavík has, for the first time, assumed a form that reflects his inner life: a fact he would not confide to anyone.

# XX

Sóla G—! She is as magnificent up close as from afar!

On their drives around town, Máni Steinn sits beside her in the front. Behind them Dr. Garibaldi Árnason sprawls on the leather-upholstered passenger seat. Between visits he leafs through reports or writes comments in a notebook. He has strictly forbidden his driver and assistant to talk so he can concentrate on his reading and jotting and hear himself think—after all, the motorcar makes enough of a racket without the addition of young people's idle chatter.

The boy watches the girl's every move:

How she holds the steering wheel; how she changes gear; how she climbs out of the vehicle and into it; how she rests her booted right foot on the running board on the driver's side while they are waiting for the doctor; how she wedges a cigarette in her plastic holder; how she inhales the smoke; how she spits a flake of tobacco from her tongue.

What impresses him most is how unaffectedly she performs all these actions; how easy it is for her to be Sóla G—.

Now he is watching her open the door of an apartment on the first floor of a house on one of the town's more prosperous streets, on the last visit of the day.

—Hello, anybody home?

Dr. Garibaldi calls in through the door. It is dark inside; an electric lamp in the stairwell casts a faint light into the hall. When no answer is heard, the doctor nods to the boy to enter first.

—There should be a man in here . . .

The boy gropes his way inside in the gloom. Curtains are pulled across all the windows, and the air is thick with the stench of vomit, blood, urine, and excrement. He pauses, takes a Lysol-soaked cloth from his pocket, and holds it up to his mouth and nose before proceeding.

There is no one in the kitchen, no one in the bedroom, no one in the bathroom, no one in the sitting room. He calls to the doctor:

—There's nobody here!

But just as the boy is about to go back into the hall he notices a strip of light in the wallpaper in the corner of the room beside the stove. On closer inspection, it turns out that there is a door concealed in the wall, which would by daylight be invisible to all except those who knew it was there.

He pushes it open. There is a compartment inside.

By the dim illumination of a reading lamp on a small desk, the boy makes out a chair and bookcase, artfully fitted into the space; walls lined with tight ranks of pictures featuring timeless motifs—Adonis and Pan, satyrs and shepherds, Saint Sebastian—and, at the edge of the pool of light, a divan bed containing a shadowy figure under a thick quilt.

The boy recognizes the man. One of his first gentlemen—the kindest of all until he met the foreigner—from whom he no longer demands payment. And who, after their last meeting, had gazed deep into his eyes and said with a catch in his voice:

*Had we but another world and time*
*Our passionate embraces were no crime.*

Dr. Garibaldi and Sóla G— appear behind the boy. The shadowy form on the divan stirs. The doctor squeezes into the compartment, pauses beside the desk on which lies a pale-blue book with two poppies on the cover, and mutters the title:

—*Mikael*.

The occupant of the compartment waves a hand at him, saying hoarsely:

—Never mind that I read Herman Bang, Doctor— be my savior and restore me to life.

The boy backs out the door before the man can spot him.

Sóla G— follows him into the passage.

There in the gloom, Máni Steinn watches as the girl places a bracing hand on his shoulder. She's well acquainted with the comings and goings of Reykjavík's evening walkers on Öskjuhlíd.

He knows all about her; she knows only this about him.

# xxi

In the course of his home visits, Dr. Garibaldi Árnason has been collecting a variety of information about the pattern of the Spanish flu, asking patients, among other things, where and how they believe they caught the disease.

A fair number think it must have been "at the pictures."

Once the doctor is convinced of the role played by the picture houses in the spread of the disease, he arranges, through the Board of Health, for the cinemas to be specially fumigated and for a public announcement to be made:

> To make people stop and think about what sort of buildings these are and what goes on inside them, and to question whether such goings-on are desirable.

For Dr. Garibaldi has long endeavored to persuade his countrymen of the dangers inherent in gawking at films.

One factor that renders film such an irresistible experience is the opportunity it affords the audience to observe other people without shame. From the safety of his seat in the darkened auditorium, the cinemagoer can, besides taking in the story that is being shown, subject the "men" and "women" on screen to a close scrutiny of the sort that would be unthinkable in society at large; on the streets, in places of employment, in cafés, in shops, in churches, or even in theaters, since in the latter the actor can, at any moment, turn on the audience and reprimand any person he feels is ogling him rather than attending to the fate of his character.

The distinction, in other words, lies in the fact that what is presented to the gaze of the cinema viewer is not real flesh-and-blood human beings but only moving pictures of people, "simulacra" created from light and shadow at the moment when the actor is filmed lending his body and emotions to the puppet that is then placed on view.

Anyone who has observed a child playing with a doll will know how intently the child examines it by touch as well as gaze. Fingers and *eyes probe the physical form with the precision of a master surgeon who has been assigned the task of dissecting a body to the bone. Every nook and cranny is inspected; nape of neck and ear, groin and instep are caressed.*

*In the same fashion, the cinema audience scrutinizes the light-puppets on the silver screen, and whether it is the curve of Asta Nielsen's back, Theda Bara's naked shoulders, Pina Menichelli's sensual eyelids, Clara Kimball Young's slim ankles, Musidora's Cupid's bow, Gunnar Tolnæs's strong fingernails, Douglas Fairbanks's firm thighs, or Max Linder's soft eyes, the body part in question and its position will become the focus of the viewer's existence and etch itself into his psyche, while the size of the image and the repeated close-ups of lips, teeth, and even tongues will exacerbate the effects until few have the strength to resist them.*

*Film is thus immoral by its very nature, transforming the actor into a fetish and fostering perversion in the viewer, who allows himself to be seduced like a moth to the flame. The difference lies in that the cinema audience's appointment is with the cold flicker of the flame rather than the searing fire itself. The moth burns up, but the viewer can, without fear, surrender to his*

*escalating desire and seek out the experience over
and over again, as is, alas, far too often the case.*
—Dr. G. Árnason, excerpt from "Cinema and
Mental Disorders," *The Nation* 23 (1916)

◆

On the evening of Tuesday, November 26—the day
that twenty-six funerals are held at the cathedral and
the coffins are interred in a single mass grave in the
northeastern corner of the cemetery—Máni Steinn and
Sóla G— pass through the auditoriums of the Old and
New Cinemas, igniting chlorine gas on the doctor's
instructions.

Dressed in black from top to toe, with black gauze
over their noses and mouths and dark goggles over their
eyes, they drip hydrochloric acid into ceramic jars containing a solution of calcium chloride, which they have
placed at intervals between the seats.

As soon as the cloud of vapor begins to rise, they
race outside into the street, closing the doors firmly
behind them.

Trembling with excitement, the boy pretends to
cough.

The greenish-yellow gas that had lately felled young
men on the battlefields of Europe now drifts and rolls
through the picture houses of Reykjavík.

# VIII

(November 30–December 1, 1918)

# VIII

(November 24–December 13, 1914)

# xxii

The first film to be shown in Reykjavík when the epidemic began to abate at the end of November, and it was thought safe to gather in public again, was called *Sister Cecilia*—"the lyrically beautiful love story of a young artist," in four parts. The proceeds of the ticket sales went to support the many children who had been left orphaned by the epidemic.

Although Máni Steinn was running a little low on cash after his busy days and nights with Sóla G— and Dr. Garibaldi Árnason—he'd had neither the energy nor the opportunity to pick up any trade—he was still sufficiently well-off to be able to invite the old lady to a show at the New Cinema.

Not that it was an easy matter to persuade her to accept the offer. First she told him it wasn't fitting for him, a child in her care, to treat her to anything. He replied that he had turned sixteen on April 23 and that it was only natural that their roles should be reversed. Such was life.

Well, then the old lady pleaded in her defense that she had already been to the *kinematograph* long ago, more than once in fact—if not three times, then at least twice—and it had always been the same damned waste of time, apart from one newsreel from Thingvellir that included a brief glimpse of Reverend Matthías Jochumsson, seated in a chair with knees spread wide, a walking stick between them and a bowler hat on his head, and that was only because the grand old man of poetry was a relative of theirs.

However, when the boy described for her the company and amenities in the more expensive seats of the New Cinema—which included an ashtray in the arm of every chair—she grudgingly agreed to accompany him.

The old lady said she had always envied the father of her landlord downstairs, who got to sit with his friends in the smoking room, wreathed in a fog of cigars, and whenever she was sent in there with soda water or a new decanter of brandy, she used to linger with them in the cloud of tobacco for as long as could be considered decent.

The film was delayed by thirty minutes while the cinemagoers offered one another their condolences, passing from row to row, neither pressing hands nor embracing but bowing their heads and repeating the same words of consolation with the variations "your daughter," "your sister," "your wife," "your husband," "your son," "your brother"—since everybody had lost someone.

A silence fell when the last member of the audience entered the auditorium. It was the teenage girl who had been shut up for thirteen days with the bodies of her mother and brother. She was led in between a nurse and an orderly from the lunatic asylum at Kleppur. From the look in her eyes it was plain that she would not understand the words of sympathy that were burning on everyone's lips.

The lights went down.

Children appeared on the screen, escorted by an angel; holy sisters knelt before a tombstone; lovers were denied a happy ending.

The screening was accompanied by Reynir Gíslason's Orchestra, and to begin with the music managed to drown out the sighing and weeping. Thick smoke rose from the more expensive seats, where the men were chain-smoking cigars in the hope that this would stifle their sobs.

When they came out afterward, the old lady wiped a tear from her eye and extracted a promise from the boy that he would never again invite her to the cinema.

# xxiii

The sun casts its rays over the town. The weather couldn't be finer; dry and not a cloud in the sky. Máni Steinn threads his way through the throng by the harbor like a needle through sackcloth until he reaches a good spot on the docks.

There the Danish warship *Islands Falk* is lying at berth, festooned with bunting from mast to mast, the Danish national flag taking pride of place over the Icelandic one.

Shortly after the cathedral bell has tolled half past eleven, the marines of the *Falcon* stand to attention on the deck of the ship, then march ashore with rifles at their shoulders and flashing bayonets. Thus equipped, they progress with regular steps from the docks to Government House, where they form an honor guard below the wall of the green. The brass band Harpa is already there with its leader, Reynir Gíslason, haggard from lack of sleep.

The thick press of people sets off in pursuit of the

column of marines, and the boy allows himself to be carried along. Most of the spectators take up position on Lækjargata, some standing in the square, others lining up on the slope to the right of Government House. He finds himself a spot in the square.

The officers of the *Falcon* approach, decked out in uniform, with the consuls of foreign powers, and together process up to the main entrance, before which stand members of the government and the Reykjavík worthies who have been invited to attend the ceremony. Among the guests, the boy spies the landlord from downstairs and the broker Gudbjörn Ólason, father of Sóla G—.

He scans the crowd for the girl and finds her on the green to the left of the building, with the families of the great and good. Today Sóla G— is dressed like Irma Vep when she was to be sent to the penal colony in Algiers: all in black down to her black leather ankle boots, a wide-brimmed black hat decorated with a black ribbon on her head; her face pale.

Outside Thomsen's Magasin a group of sailors from the *Falcon* stand and marvel at how subdued the Icelanders seem on what should be a day of national rejoicing. They are right that in most respects the gathering bears more resemblance to a funeral than to the birth of a sovereign state. People hang their heads; many of the women's faces are hidden behind mourning veils; the men wear black bands on their arms.

At a quarter to twelve the brass band strikes up "Ancient Land of Ice," and men doff their hats during the performance—which proves to be so marred by lack of practice that it is torture to the ears—and afterward the minister of finance ascends the steps before Government House and embarks on the solemn oration.

As the minister speaks of the hearts of the nation, of their late leader, of the culmination of a hundred-year struggle, of braving the stormy seas, and of the honor of the national flag, the boy can't help thinking that this is exactly the sort of occasion at which the Vampires would strike. For example, by firing a shell at it from their fearsome portable cannon. But of course that would merely be a diversion. In the chaos created by the act of sabotage, other members of the criminal gang would dynamite the vaults of the National Bank and break into the state treasury—then escape the country by seaplane.

Where would they place the cannon? Well, they could disguise themselves as French missionaries and rent rooms on the top floor of Thomsen's Magasin. That would provide a clear line of sight.

Turning to look over his shoulder, the boy examines the store from roof to ground, at which point his eye alights on the sailors. One of them, a muscular fellow with a blond mustache, catches sight of him as well.

On the steps the minister brings his speech to a close.

And as the swallowtail flag of the new sovereign state of Iceland is hoisted up the lofty pole by Government House and the *Islands Falk* fires a twenty-one-gun salute in its honor, the eyes of boy and sailor meet.

# xxiv

A fanfare of horns carries through the door: "Rise, thou youthful flag of Iceland!"

Inside the hardware store of Thomsen's Magasin, boy and sailor are locked in a fevered embrace—as they exchange deep kisses, the boy tastes the Dane's vinegar-sweet tongue and wonders briefly if he himself tastes of coffee—he'd led the sailor behind the French stores into Kolasund, the alley where he sometimes takes gentlemen after midnight to service them in the shadow of the latrine, and it just so happened that the warehouse door had been left open.

They remove their winter jackets without breaking off their kiss. The sailor tugs the braces off the boy's shoulders, pulls his shirt tails out of his waistband, and inserts his right hand under the shirt, stroking the boy's back, while holding the nape of his neck with the left. The boy clutches the sailor's buttocks in both hands, pressing him close as he thrusts his own hips forward, so their rock-hard penises rub together through their clothes. The sailor moves his hand around to the boy's chest, pinches a nipple between thumb and forefinger, and twists it.

The warehousemen are standing in the square in front of the building, a stone's throw from the sailor's shipmates, listening with them to the captain of the *Falcon* as he passes on to the assembled crowd the greetings of King Christian X, his parliament and nation. Standing beside the lathe, meanwhile, surrounded by chains of all sizes, by bolts and nails, tins of paint, hammers and pliers, overalls and boots, the boy and the Dane continue their lovemaking.

The sailor eases the boy's trousers down his thighs and drops to his knees. Holding the boy's cock, he licks his balls, rolling the testicles around with his tongue before running it from the root to the purple dome, which he tickles with his mustache before closing his lips around it.

The brass band plays "King Christian."

The boy leans back against the lathe while the sailor sucks him, supporting himself with one hand while playing with the Dane's blond hair with the other.

Nine cheers of hurrah resound outside in the square.

Detaching himself from the sailor, the boy raises him to his feet, unbuttons his fly, puts his hand inside his underpants, takes hold of his stiff member, pulls down the foreskin, runs the tip of his thumb over the swollen dome, clasps it, and, rubbing gently, spreads the bead of moisture that is squeezed out of the top.

The sailor sticks his index and middle fingers in his mouth, wetting them well, then runs his hand under the boy's balls, sliding his fingers along the ridge to the anus, where he begins to open a way for himself. The boy, emitting a low groan, tightens his grip on the sailor's cock and rubs harder.

The ceremony before Government House is drawing to a close.

The boy turns to the lathe and bends over it. The sailor enters him.

First the Danish national anthem, "There Is a Lovely Land," is sung, then the Icelandic, "O God of Our Country."

It seems the cheers will never end.

In the very instant that Máni Steinn climaxes, he feels the sailor's hot seed spurting inside him—and the warehouse door is kicked open.

There's a despairing cry in Danish from the doorway:

—*Mogens, what the hell are you doing?*

Seconded in Icelandic:

—What the devil is this filth?

The latter words are accompanied by a blow from a clenched fist that knocks the boy senseless.

# IX

(December 5–6, 1918)

# XXV

—Put him out of his misery, I say . . . Easy enough to hide his body . . . the mortuaries are full of nameless wretches . . . Give him to the medical students to skin . . . they've been snapping up the bodies of prostitutes . . . Nothing left of Good-time Jóka but the bare bones . . . split among them for souvenirs . . . the nights they spent with her before she went down with the flu . . . Ha-ha . . . Put him out of his misery, I say, put him out of his misery . . .

Máni Steinn has his ear pressed to the door of the room where he is being held, trying to make out the conversation on the other side. No one backs up the shouted suggestion of the agitated individual who wants to "put him out of his misery." Nor is the boy alarmed by such talk. He has realized that the men meeting to decide his fate are not the type. The agitated man is shouting more to himself than to the others:

—Drown him like a rabid cur . . . The bloody brat's got the eyes of a sheep-killing dog . . .

But the other men's unenthusiastic response to the idea that they should murder and fillet the boy does not make them innocent of the wish to solve the problem by the quickest possible means.

The last thing people want to see at the dawn of the Icelandic sovereign state are headlines in the domestic or Danish press about a sodomy scandal in Reykjavík.

The country would be a laughingstock in Denmark; opponents of its new sovereign status would make capital out of the incident for ridicule and derision in the snide manner that is the trademark of the Danes; declaring good riddance to this nation of "up the assers" who are incapable of leaving Danish sailors alone—why, they might even dub the country Assland and choose a crude flag for it as a mockery. Yes, the Danish papers can be relied on to hold the Icelander responsible for the perverted act, and to whitewash the sailor, although he had of course already been badly infected with the vice before he ever came to the country with the *Falcon*. Fortunately, the captain of the warship is supporting their decision to hush up the affair. The vessel has left port and the sailor will be subjected to Danish naval discipline.

No, the morale of the townspeople is so low after the blows of recent weeks that they cannot cope with any further setbacks. The clouds of unnatural foreign practices must not be permitted to cast a shadow over the warming sun that rose in the sorrowful hearts of the nation on December 1.

It should also be borne in mind that the offender lives in the same house as a respectable citizen, an influential member of the Socialist Party, who has recently lost his son.


Then the boy hears a voice he recognizes.

Dr. Garibaldi Árnason takes the floor.

—It's clear that the lad is not like other people . . . a *homosexual* . . . given over to the lamentable vice of wishing to engage in erotic acts with his own sex . . . revolting to other people . . . Now we know that in such cases . . . the body is no less infected than the mind . . . a specific and multiple disorder in the body's glandular development and functioning . . . His perversion compounded by satyriasis . . . In other respects a diligent lad . . . can testify to that . . . plucky . . . A tricky matter . . . Hardly any cases known in this country . . . hasn't become established . . . will proliferate if . . . My theory . . . a word of warning . . . men are rendered more susceptible to *homosexuality* by overindulgence in films . . .

The doctor is interrupted:

— . . . do you say, Gudbjörn?

The answer is firm:

— . . . have to get him . . .

This comment creates a stir among those attending the meeting, who all start talking at once, such is their solidarity in the face of this abomination.

# XXVI

Máni Steinn has no idea where he is. He came to his senses in this room and has been here ever since.

A woman he has never seen before brings him food. She is dressed like a nurse but doesn't behave like one. And the room itself does not resemble a hospital ward. It contains a sofa, two armchairs and two dining chairs, a coffee table and a basket of newspapers, a decorated screen with a stool and a clothes stand behind it, and, opening off the room, a cloakroom with a washbasin and WC.

The room is windowless but has electric lighting, and the boy guesses that he has been there for three or four days and nights. He sleeps on the sofa, covered by a blanket, with an embroidered cushion under his head, and for the first two days he slept almost continuously. He suspects that he has been drugged.

To prevent the boy from escaping, the nurse takes the precaution of placing the food tray on the floor outside the door, then knocking, opening it a crack and waiting for him to go to the opposite end of the room before widening the gap and pushing the tray inside with the toe of her shoe, then slamming the door shut. Rather than fetching the tray, she brings a new one every time, so a pile of trays and dirty crockery is building up in the room.

The room has two other doors besides the one that leads to the WC: the one at which he has been eavesdropping and through which the nurse delivers his tray, and another that has not yet been opened but from under which comes an agreeable odor of disinfectant.

He has tried peering through the keyholes, but both contain keys since the room is, of course, locked.

◆

There is a knock on the door; the key is turned. The boy moves to the far end of the room. But instead of the nurse four men walk in.

He recognises three of them: the landlord from downstairs, Dr. Garibaldi Árnason, and Gudbjörn Ólason, but he can't place the fourth, good at faces though he is.

Gudbjörn acts as spokesman, and once all four are seated he explains to the boy the plans they have for his future. It is in his interests to comply. He must understand that if this hadn't happened in such special circumstances, he would be on his way to prison or worse by now. Dr. Garibaldi pats the boy's knee, firmly and encouragingly; the landlord from downstairs keeps his eyes lowered; the fourth man snorts.

Finally, Gudbjörn asks if there is anything in particular, apart from his clothes, that Máni Steinn would like them to fetch from the old lady—he calls her by her full name—who will be told that the boy has been given a place on a trawler.

The boy replies that under his pillow is a red scarf that he would be glad to have.

When they are leaving, the shadow of the door falls on the fourth man just as he turns back and calls out:

—But, but, shouldn't he, shouldn't we . . . ?

And then the boy recognizes the voice of the man who wanted to "put him out of his misery," who is none other than the shifty gentleman he sucked off on the slope of Öskjuhlíd the night the Katla eruption began.

He smiles at the man. That shuts him up.

◆

The boy lies down on the sofa and in no time he is asleep.

He dreams of antelopes.

# XXVII

—Máni, Máni Steinn . . .

    The boy feels a touch on his shoulder:

—Máni . . .

    Sóla G— is kneeling beside the sofa.

◆

They emerge from the clinic where the boy has been held and he discovers that he's in the largest building he has ever entered. A whitewashed corridor; black-varnished doors on either side as far as the eye can see; a ceiling three times the normal height; highly polished linoleum; and great spherical ceiling lights that recede in a row down the corridor like a fading echo.

    Máni Steinn feels an urge to shout.

    The staircase alone would make an impressive structure. As if hewn from rock, the steps descend and vanish into the darkness of the lower floors. And from the wide stairwell rises a tower of wrought iron: the elevator shaft.

Sóla G— is at home here. Her father's office is on the first floor. She presses a button beside the elevator doors.

A clank is heard from the top of the shaft.

The mechanism comes to life and with a reassuring hum begins to drag the elevator up to where they are standing.

◆

Sóla G— lends the boy her hand and helps him out of a window on the top floor of the huge Nathan & Olsen building. It is pitch-dark.

—Stay close to me.

The boy picks his way after the girl's silhouette, first along a walkway above the eaves, then diagonally up the sloping roof until they reach the top. His head swims, and Sóla G— tells him to straddle the ridge. Seated like this, he shuffles after her to the tower, where she helps him to his feet.

—I thought you might like to see this before you leave.

From the roof of the largest building ever con-structed in Iceland—it is a whole six stories high—there is a view north to the Snæfellsjökull Glacier and south to the Reykjanes Peninsula with the pyramid form of Mount Keilir.

There is a view of Reykjavík too, darkened by the shortages—the houses look like the lumps of coal that people can only dream of.

Máni Steinn gazes out at the spit of Laugarnes, the only place in town left untouched by the epidemic, and suddenly the thought strikes him that before he and Sóla G— say goodbye for the last time there is something he must tell her about himself.

He points to an imposing wooden building on the spit.

—That's where I lived for the first year after I came to town.

The girl is thrown.

—At the Leper Hospital?

◆

The freighter *Sterling* is lying at anchor in the harbor.

Two passengers are to leave with her at dawn.

The boy is one. The other is an Englishman, who for more than a month has been waiting out the Spanish flu at the Merchant's House in the village of Eyrarbakki on the south coast. And he's surprisingly kind for a peg leg—as the old lady would put it—since he has agreed to escort the boy to London.

There he will be received by an Icelander who knows all the ropes—the playwright Haraldur Hamar.

Máni Steinn laughs; black wings beat wildly in his breast.

X

(July 9, 1929)

# xxviii

There is a cosmopolitan air to the group who appear at the telegram counter of the Reykjavík Post Office one July afternoon in 1929.

These are the trio associated with the Pool Group—the director Kenneth Macpherson, the poet Robert Herring, and the novelist Annie Winifred Ellerman, who has adopted the pen name of Bryher—and M. Peter Carlson, their assistant and interpreter on their Icelandic tour. The purpose of their visit to the country is to record footage for an experimental film.

Shortly before leaving England they held a screening in an art gallery of their second short film, *Monkeys' Moon*, and celebrated the first issue of the fourth year of their cinema journal, *Close Up*, published and edited by Macpherson and Bryher, to which Herring has from the outset been one of the key contributors. The journal proclaims itself the first in the world to treat cinema as a fine art that calls for experimentation and psychological inquiry. It also crusades against censorship of all kinds.

Like their friends in the French surrealist movement, the group is fascinated by Freud's theories and methods. They believe that with focused and audacious cinematography—scratching and drawing directly onto film, irrational montages, superimposition, changes of speed, close-ups of objects and body parts, intercuts between images of animals and people, the subversion of a linear plot—it is possible to re-create the complex life of the unconscious and free the individual from obsolete ethical norms and psychological inhibitions.

Their goal is the psychoanalysis of the masses and the liberation of society through film.

Two of the foursome enjoy a permissive lifestyle that would be unthinkable to the inhabitants of the country they are visiting, not because they live a life of luxury courtesy of Bryher's vast fortune—she is the daughter of the shipping magnate John Ellerman, the wealthiest man in the history of Britain, lives in an exclusive villa in Switzerland's Montreux, and is a patron of artists from all over Europe—nor because they move in a world where friendships can be destroyed by a difference of opinion about a minute-long close-up or a single word in a poem, but because Bryher and Macpherson entered into their marriage solely in order to adopt the daughter of Hilda Doolittle, a.k.a. H.D., the American poet and member of Pool, with whom both are having an affair.

The telegram assistant cannot guess from the appearance or behavior of the group that they are experimentalists in more than just literature and film. Macpherson's and Herring's vivacity doesn't strike him as the slightest bit odd—after all, high spirits are perfectly normal in those who have just disembarked in a new country; his attention is mainly drawn to Bryher's short hair, since his own girlfriend has been talking about getting a bob.

The group's reason for visiting the telephone exchange is for Bryher to send a wire to H.D.—due to a *crise de nerfs*, she has not come with them to Iceland but remained at home in London in her flat on Sloane Street—for so passionate is their love that they write to each other daily when parted by land or sea.

Carlson makes the arrangements and waits while Bryher reads the message to the pop-eyed assistant:

"DEAR CAT—STOP—SAFE IN THULE—STOP—
LOVE FIDO"

Once they have emerged from the post office, Carlson asks his traveling companions to excuse him because he is still unsteady on his legs after their voyage around the cape of Reykjanes and he doesn't feel up to attending afternoon tea with Snæbjörn Jónsson, owner of the English Bookshop, and his wife, A. Florence Westcott. Before he takes leave of the trio, they agree to meet first thing the next day in the saloon of the S.S. *Arcadian*.

They will be leaving port early on this large cruise liner, which literary types like to call *Pan* after the most famous of Arcadia's sons.

The footage the Pool Group have come to Iceland to shoot is to include seals, and they are hoping to find some up north.

# XXIX

Shortly after the locals and their guests have sat down to dinner, M. Peter Carlson walks through the cemetery gate on the corner of Sudurgata and Sólvallagata. At the top of the slope are the graves of those who died in the Spanish flu.

The rowan saplings planted in 1919 have grown tall.

Their flowers light up the evening like a myriad white suns.

A little farther to the west Carlson finds the grave he has come to visit. It is marked by a white marble slab, which he'd had engraved in England and sent over to the cemetery:

KARMILLA MARIUSDOTTIR
*JUNE 14, 1833
†SEPTEMBER 6, 1924
REST IN PEACE

He was six years old when he was placed in the care of Karmilla Maríusdóttir. Whether she was his only living relative or the only one who dared to take him in, he doesn't know. She was seventy-five, and informed him that she was his great-grandmother's sister and that he mustn't expect to be with her for long as she should have been dead years ago.

He had a mother and remembers her as well as it is possible to remember a person one hardly ever saw or touched. He retains no memories of anyone else. If he ever had a father or siblings, a grandfather or grandmother, they are lost. And since the old woman never mentioned them, he never asked.

Yet he has a faint memory of a girl feeding him blueberries. He can sometimes feel the berries on his lips. She could have been his sister—though it's just as likely that he was never fed blueberries at all.

The first years of his life were tied to one person and one place:

His mother and the door of her room.

Below the middle of the door was a hatch that opened from the outside. Through it he used to see his mother at mealtimes and "when she was allowed to have him by her." Then the hatch was left open for a while and the woman used to sit beside it and talk to her child.

He understands now that his mother was already

suffering from leprosy when she gave birth to him. By the time he first remembers sitting on the footstool outside the hatch, she had taken to covering her face with a veil and wearing gloves on her hands.

Once, she allowed him to see her. He can still summon up the image of her gentle face as it appeared to him through the bottom of the glass that she asked him to hold to his eye.

If he did anything else for those first five years apart from sit on that footstool, he cannot say. It was only when he was mounted on a horse and taken away that he saw the farm where they lived for the first time. Once they had crossed the river, he turned in the arms of the man who was holding him and saw the turf-roofed farm at the foot of a high mountain with four peaks.

Their journey ended at the Leper Hospital on Laugarnes.

After a year had passed and it was certain that he had not been infected, he was sent into town to Karmilla Maríusdóttir.

The next thing the old lady said, after predicting her imminent death, was that he must never tell a soul what had happened to his mother and "never, never, never" that he himself had been in the men's ward at the Leper Hospital.

And he answered:

—But I'm not a man, I'm a child . . .

# XXX

Toward the eastern end of Lindargata, right by Vita-
torg Square, there is a two-story house, clad in corru-
gated iron and painted in bolder colors than any of its
neighbors. The roof is black, the side walls and gables
purple, the woodwork maroon, and the window mul-
lions white.

A charabanc is parked in the drive leading to a
workshop that is decorated in the same colors as the
house. The sign painted on its sides reads:

SÓLBORG GUDBJÖRNSDÓTTIR—HOUSE PAINTER
TELEPHONE: 323—FOR DECORATING IN ANY
COLOR

Leaning against the workshop wall on the garden side
is an old Indian motorcycle—its red varnish peeling, its
tires flat—and beside it stands a gleaming Triumph
Model Q.

The windows facing the street are at head height

and one of them is open. The curtain has been sucked out of it and flaps in the evening breeze. There is the sound of female voices inside.

M. Peter Carlson walks along the sandy shore in the direction of Laugarnes.

He's glad he didn't give in to the temptation to knock on the door of the purple house:

Sóla G— lives on untouched in his memory.

The last few years have been good to him. He trained as an electrician and has had plenty to do assisting lighting technicians and cameramen on films. His job title is Best Boy—in other words, he's still a boy, though he's now twenty-seven years old.

He rents a small flat in Chelsea with Richard "Buddy" Williams, a printer of whom he is very fond. Williams produces books of poetry and other slim volumes in small print runs of exceptionally high quality. That is how they became acquainted with the Pool Group, though Carlson had already been aware of their existence and had noticed H.D. at the parties he attended with Haraldur Hamar when he first arrived in England.

Carlson goes to all the films that come to London. Naturally, he has already seen Josef von Sternberg's *Underworld*, which is showing at Reykjavík's Old Cinema this evening. Bryher and Macpherson do not share his enthusiasm for Sternberg's crime pictures—they prefer the psychological dramas of G. W. Pabst—but he recognizes the debt Sternberg owes to Feuillade's *Les Vampires* and *Fantomas*, which is filmmaking to his taste.

In the hall of his and Buddy's flat on Tite Street hangs a sign: BEWARE OF FALLING COCONUTS.

That's their kind of humor.


Carlson is only fifty yards short of the Leper Hospital when he experiences a sudden sensation of weightlessness. Glancing at his hands, he discovers that he can see right through them. He gropes for his body and finds that he is clutching at thin air. He can't feel a thing apart from the wingbeats where his heart used to be.


A middle-aged man comes around the corner of the hospital. This is Sigurdur Ásgrímsson, a farmer from Dæli on Lake Hópsvatn, who has been a patient here since he fell ill with the disease six years ago.

For an instant he thinks a young man is standing before him, but at the next moment a black butterfly appears, bigger than any he has set eyes on before. It flutters up to him and settles on the stump of the ring finger of his right hand. A thought crosses his mind:

"My Gísli would appreciate this."

Gísli, the fourth of his seven children, is a boy of

thirteen who has been employed on a fishing boat on the island of Málmey ever since the family was broken up.

Neither of them knows that in ten years' time Gísli will have a son named Sigurdur Ásgrímur, or that his sixth child will be the son Steinólfur Sævar, known all his life as Bósi.

And it will be in memory of Bósi—sailor, alcoholic, booklover, socialist, and gay—who will die of AIDS in the month of May 1993, that Sigurdur Ásgrímur's eldest son, Sigurjón, will sit down to write the story of Máni Steinn, the boy who never was.

# ACKNOWLEDGMENTS

Special thanks are due to A. S. Byatt and Neel Mukherjee for their inspiration and support.

# PERMISSIONS ACKNOWLEDGMENTS

Epigraph: Translation of Robert Desnos's poem "À la mystérieuse" ("To the One of Mystery"), 1926, by Bill Zavatsky.

*Billy* by Anonymous, quoted on page 26, is taken from the ninth reprint of *Poems of the Great War*, published by the Macmillan Company, 1916.

Images on pages 71–72 are stills from Episode 6 of *Les Vampires*, a film by Louis Feuillade, Production Gaumont, 1915.

Extract on pages 83–84, translation of an article published in *Morgunbladid*, November 17, 1918.

Photograph on page 143 of Robert Herring, Kenneth Macpherson, and Bryher, taken on their 1929 trip. Photographer unknown.

Photograph on page 144 of Steinólfur Sævar Gíslason Geirdal, detail of a larger picture published in *Thjódviljinn*, March 11, 1987. Photograph by Einar Ólason.

## A NOTE ABOUT THE AUTHOR

Born in Reykjavik in 1962, Sjón is a celebrated Icelandic novelist. He won the Nordic Council's Literary Prize (the Nordic countries' equivalent of the Man Booker Prize) for his novel *The Blue Fox*, and his novel *From the Mouth of the Whale* was short-listed for both the International IMPAC Dublin Literary Award and the Independent Foreign Fiction Prize. Also a poet, librettist, and lyricist, he has published nine poetry collections and written four opera librettos, as well as lyrics for various artists. In 2001 he was nominated for an Oscar for his lyrics for the film *Dancer in the Dark*. Sjón's novels have been published in thirty-five languages.